Jacob's
First Ski Holiday

Nick Robinson
Illustrator Stefan Bast

Jacob rushed out from school on a cold and rainy day.

"Mummy, Mummy," Jacob said excitedly.

"Today, my teacher told us that the whole school will break up for school holidays soon. Does that mean we are going on holiday?" asked Jacob.

"Yes Jacob, we are going on a ski holiday," said Mummy.

"But Mummy! I don't know how to ski!" said Jacob, looking worried!

"Don't worry Jacob, you will have ski lessons," said Mummy.

That evening Jacob fell asleep dreaming of glistening white snow.

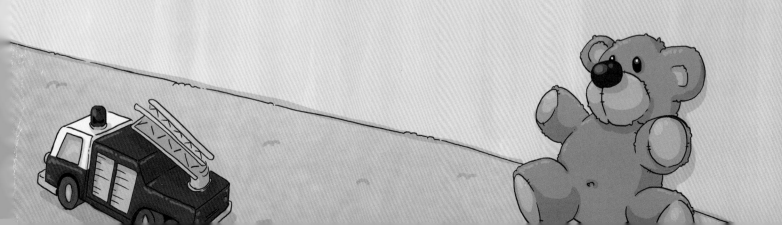

Two weeks later, Jacob and his family were packing their suitcases for their ski holiday. Jacob always liked to pack his own suitcase.

"All packed," Jacob told his Daddy.

"Are you sure you have everything Jacob?" asked Daddy.

"Of course - I have my swimming trunks, swim goggles, clothes and my teddy," Jacob explained.

"Jacob, we're going on a ski holiday remember! You will be freezing cold wearing your swimming trunks skiing! We need to pack some ski clothes," said Daddy.

"We will need gloves, a woolly hat, thermals, ski goggles and a ski suit," explained Daddy, as he placed the ski clothes into Jacob's suitcase.

Jacob was so excited that he struggled to sleep, he knew that when he woke up in the morning they would be travelling to the mountains on holiday.

The journey was quicker than Jacob expected. He thought it would be a long looooong way to the mountains, but it was just a short flight. It seemed like no time at all before they were in the bus, driving up the snowy mountain road.

"Wow!" Jacob shouted. "Mummy, Daddy, look at all the snow!!"

He had never seen so much snow before!

It was already dark when they arrived and all the family were in bed not long after. They needed a good night's sleep before their first day skiing. Jacob went to sleep dreaming about his first ski lesson!

The next morning they woke up to the beeping sound of machines called piste bashers flattening the slopes ready for the skiers.

BEEP BEEP BEEP

They had to meet their ski instructor at 9:15 near the "magic carpet", so Jacob and his family picked up all their ski equipment and off they went.

An instructor called Kenny, who had been teaching children to ski for many years, greeted them. Jacob was suddenly nervous and stood by his Daddy's side.

Jacob was skiing for the first time, so he was in a beginners group with five other boys and girls. Everybody was nervous · but excited!

All the Mummies and Daddies said goodbye and left to go skiing, some of them even had lessons of their own to go to.

The first thing they had to do was learn how to put their skis on, so one by one Kenny showed them how to do it.

"Toe in first, then click the heel down."

CLICK, CLACK, POW and all the skis were on.

Next, they had to learn how to walk on the snow whilst wearing their skis.

"Right Jacob, you need to move one foot at a time, being very careful not to cross your skis!" explained Kenny. After a few tries Jacob had it!

"I can do it, I can do it Kenny!" shouted Jacob excitedly.

Before long all the children were walking round in a big circle, having lots of fun. It felt strange at first, but with Kenny's help they quickly got used to having skis on their feet.

Before using a ski lift, they had to learn how to walk up the slippery snowy slope. This sounded silly, but once Kenny showed them how to do it, everybody found it easy!

Kenny explained: "If you try and walk up the hill going forwards you will just slide backwards! You must point your skis across the slope and then take one step at a time, up the mountain."

Jacob listened really carefully and walked sideways up the hill, just like a crab. He was first up to where Kenny was waiting.

Kenny was very pleased with all the boys and girls: "Well done Jacob, now you can point your skis down the slope, bend your knees and have a slide!"

"Weeeeeeeee," said Jacob.

"I'm skiing, that was so much fun!"

And up Jacob walked again.

Once everyone had practised, it was time to use the "magic carpet".

"Now we must learn how to snow plough. This is how we slow ourselves down and as soon as everyone can do it we will go and explore the mountain."

"Turn your feet inwards and move your legs apart, making your skis go in the shape of a pizza slice. This is called a snow plough," explained Kenny.

Once everyone had got used to snow ploughing, Kenny asked the children to follow him. They skied in a big train down the slope copying all of his turns.

"Is everyone ready to go and explore the rest of the mountain?" shouted Kenny excitedly.

"Yesssss!" said Jacob, throwing his hands in the air.

This is when the fun really started!

Kenny took them over to a bubble lift, they all jumped into the same bubble and up they went.

"Woohooo it's like a rollercoaster," one of the children said.

From the bubble, high above the slopes, they could see all the skiers whizzing down the slopes below. All the children were trying to spot their Mummies and Daddies skiing.

When they reached the top of the mountain, Kenny told them they were going to be skiing down a green run.

"Make sure you all follow me, no overtaking!" Kenny told them.

All the children huddled off like penguins and followed Kenny down the mountain. They weaved down the hill through the trees, until they arrived at a beautiful wooden chalet.

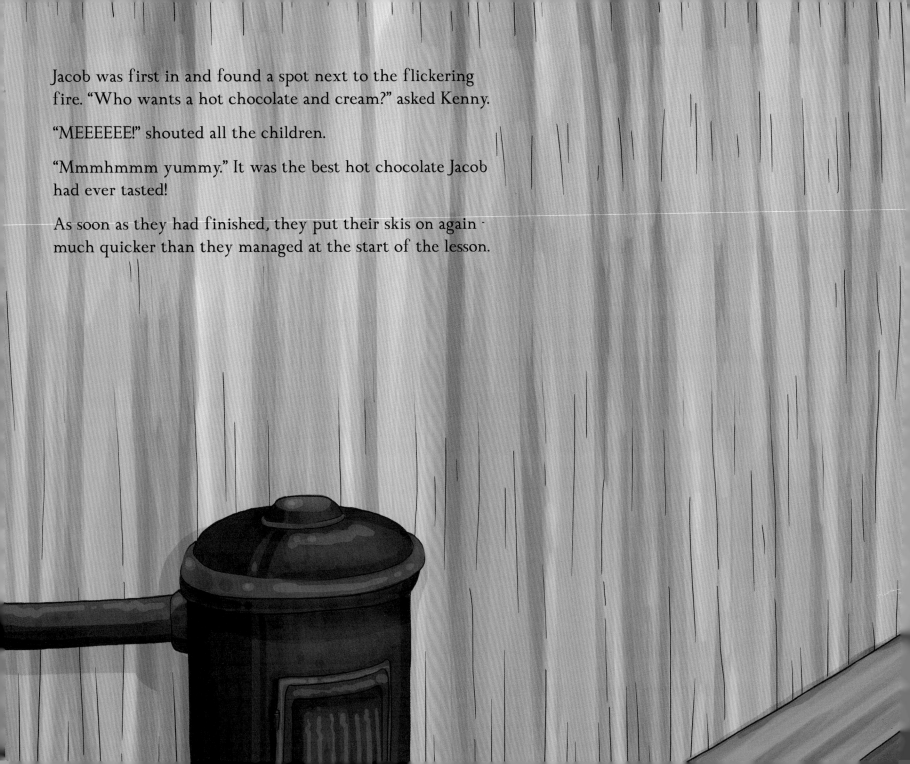

Jacob was first in and found a spot next to the flickering fire. "Who wants a hot chocolate and cream?" asked Kenny.

"MEEEEEE!" shouted all the children.

"Mmmhmmm yummy." It was the best hot chocolate Jacob had ever tasted!

As soon as they had finished, they put their skis on again - much quicker than they managed at the start of the lesson.

Jacob couldn't believe he was skiing, as he followed Kenny and the other children down the mountain. He kept watching other skiers coming past and hoped he could ski like them one day.

It was time for the ski lesson to finish and Jacob couldn't wait to see his Mummy and Daddy, to tell them all about his morning.

Kenny told them: "I will see you all tomorrow morning, everyone did wonderfully well today! Tomorrow we can go and explore more runs on the mountain and maybe even try a jump!"

Jacob spotted his Mummy and ran over to her: "Mummy, Mummy! Skiing is so much fun, can we stay here forever?"

Mummy laughed and said to Jacob: "We can't, but you get to go skiing again in the morning!"

Jacob shouted: "Thank you Kenny, see you tomorrow," and waved goodbye.

Later that afternoon Jacob looked out of his hotel window and noticed something falling from the sky.

"It's snowing!! Pleeeaase can I go outside and play Mummy?" Jacob asked.

"Of course Jacob, let's all go out together."

Jacob spent hours outside building snowmen and sledging down the hill. Then the sun had started to set and it was time to head back inside for dinner and a good night's sleep before the next day's adventures started.

Just a couple of hours later and Jacob was all tucked
up in bed. He couldn't wait to fall asleep and wake up
in the morning, so he could go skiing again.

He gave his Mummy and Daddy a kiss goodnight and
closed his eyes, he drifted off to sleep thinking of the
white snow falling outside his window.

THE END